THE SWAN WHISPERER

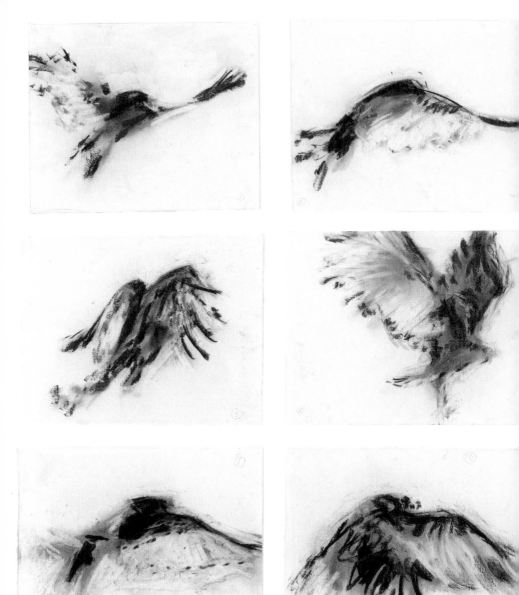

MARLENE VAN NIEKERK

The Swan Whisperer:
An inaugural lecture

Translated from the Afrikaans
by Marius Swart and the author

The Cahiers
Series

CENTER FOR WRITERS & TRANSLATORS
THE AMERICAN UNIVERSITY OF PARIS

—

SYLPH EDITIONS

H ONOURABLE RECTOR, Dean, dear colleagues, friends, and family: What does one teach when one is a teacher of Creative Writing? The true? The good? The beautiful? Should one teach criticism, fantasy, or faith? What is the use of literature? What is its place on the greater canvas of human endeavours? And perhaps I should also ask: Can a story offer consolation?

I do not pretend to have answers to these questions. What I shall share with you tonight is the experience that made such questions irrelevant to me. It concerns a correspondence with a student – I shall call him *Kasper Olwagen*; or rather it concerns some letters he sent to me, letters to which I barely replied.

The sand is slipping through the hourglass. Perhaps some clarity may be reached by my exposing the entire episode to a critical audience such as yourselves?

The first missive from Kasper was a letter – if one may call it that, at sixty-seven pages. Let me read you its first paragraphs.

Bed B, Ward 1002, Intensive Care Unit
Academisch Medisch Centrum, Amsterdam
24 February 2002
Dear Professor Van Niekerk,

    As you may deduce from the above address, I am in a situation of personal crisis. Ruled paper, leaking ball-point, intravenous drip in the back of my hand, catheter in the lily of my urinary tract. I know that such a letter is the last thing you would expect of me, after years of reading my bone-dry manuscripts. I know also that you prefer to keep your students at a distance, not to have to read their boring and poorly veiled self-revelations. But the time of reckoning (tempus fugit!) hath come. I know you well enough to be certain that what I have to say will not bore you. But as you always maintain: 'No desire without technique,' and 'No truth without rhetoric.'

    Cut to the chase, Kasper! Shorter sentences, Olwagen! Suggestion, not interpretation! Stick to the knitting, orient your reader in space and time! Lie, but don't deceive!

    Against any intimation of deceit, let me defend myself in advance. Despite having awakened only three days ago from what the nursing staff call a 'babbling delirium,' and despite still being in the intensive care unit under observation, I possess concrete evidence that I have not dreamt up what occurred. I have in my possession the coat, the shoes, perhaps the tongue, of someone other than myself. But let me not mislead you: I have no energy for tall tales at present. If my tribulations in Amsterdam have had any effect, they have finally healed me of my ambition, precisely, to write fiction. Accept this, then, as official notice: I am dropping my studies. Sorry about the waste of your precious time. But might this letter also act as compensation? I would not be surprised if you were to use my story for one of your own dark designs.

Kasper Olwagen was thirty years old when he wrote this letter, with a degree in philosophy: slight, pale, with intense eyes, a high forehead, a delicate mouth; well-groomed (especially his hands), a skin sensitive to sun and cold. His movements seemed tentative, his nostrils twitched constantly as though inspecting the air for imponderable hints. He appeared brittle. His classmates nicknamed him *Mister Xenos*. He was intelligent, obsessive, withdrawn, a bookworm, falling into a slight lisp whenever nervous or excited. There was something old-fashioned in his manner. For appointments he wore a waistcoat, a ruby-red bowtie, and his fountain-pen was visible in the inside pocket of his jacket. He would remove it when he wanted to make a note in his small, black notebook: hesitantly, as though he wished first to touch his heart.

On my recommendation, Mister Xenos was to spend three months overseas during the local summer recess, over Christmas 2001 to 2002. I had heard, quite by accident, of a bursary of the Stichting Literaire Activiteiten Moederstad – the mother city in this case being not Cape Town but Amsterdam – which offered funding and accommodation to a young, unpublished writer from South Africa. Exposure to a stimulating environment, along with pressure from his Dutch hosts, might help him produce something tangible; previous pressure from me had only been counterproductive. He was one of those students simply unable to complete his writing project for the M.A. course, hampered as he was by extended episodes of writer's block. I suspected that what inhibited him was oversensitivity to criticism, alienation from his peers, confusion about the South African reality, perfectionism, hypochondria. He suffered from what he called a 'murmuring heart' – suppressed libido, I suspected.

On the day I received his letter I read only the first two paragraphs before setting it aside. I was into the home stretch of a novel I was writing, the final revisions, surrounded by the usual chaos accompanying that stage in the process – frozen meals from Nice and Easy, dirty dishes, a mouse in the kitchen, squirrels inside the roof, garden overgrown, wrist inflamed – and I saw no sense in spending more time on a difficult student who clearly wished to drop out. In the five years since first enrolling, Kasper Olwagen had invariably handed his work in late, pieces burdened with excessive detail, freighted with information and illustration, in which absolutely nothing ever happened. 'User manual!' I would comment. 'Delete unnecessary details.' Kasper's further problem was his profundity. He frequently discussed big ethical questions: *What is a good person?* Or *How is a good person to live?* And he did so always in the form of wholly indigestible allegories. Alongside

Windhoek is my
Death
Windhoek is my
Death
Windhoek is my
Death
August 1904

Entkräftung

14 Hunger

15

20 Durst

11 District 30 Cam

36 Durst

1904

1905 Habgier

41a Hunger 41

Unerhört!

Durst

each of his moralistic figures I wrote in the margin: 'Delete the ideas!' He simply could not achieve a narrative resolution of meaning and minutiae. Kasper Olwagen should be a philosopher, I thought, not a writer.

Yet here was this letter from Amsterdam, and its introductory paragraph was quivering with appetisers. Why did I not read any further?

I dropped a card into the mail, rather: 'Speedy recovery, and thanks for your entertaining letter. I shall notify University Administration. All best.'

Two weeks later his letter resurfaced from beneath a stack of papers, and I thought to myself: Let's keep this on file, just in case. As I was punching holes into it, the following paragraph caught my eye – I was irked by its impertinence:

Professor, I do not yet understand everything that has happened – and is still happening – to me in this city. I am astonished here in my hospital bed, as you will be by the end of this letter, even though you are employed at an institute of higher learning where there is no longer any place for astonishment, for fear or fascination, reverence or awe. I am returning to South Africa in one month's time. To whom else could I possibly confide this forewarning of my fate? As you know, I am unattached. Unattached! How dubious, this concept. An invisible string connects us all, and it is only a matter of time before we come face to face, asking: Haven't we met somewhere before? Despite all your prescriptiveness and indifference, I have always experienced you as a kind of mother, even if you're not brimming with the milk of human kindness. Now let me get to the point.

Point? What point? I thought, as I flicked through three deleted pages, each line carefully crossed out so the words were still legible. Words I had to peruse, of course: a minutely detailed description of the accommodation in Amsterdam that I had helped him to obtain. 'User manual,' I was thinking again. Here is the gist of it.

It was a writer's paradise. Even lying here in intensive care, I recall it vividly, an apartment on the fourth floor, close to Amsterdam harbour at the upper end of the Geldersekade. Three double windows with small panes in the living room made of thick, antique glass, slightly discoloured and full of bubbles and flaws. To the north, a view of the seventeenth-century gabling on the quay. To the east, the former docks, where two bright yellow cranes were constantly lifting and lowering building materials. With my binoculars ('Always take along your binoculars,' you had said) I could make out the name Liebherr *on their masts. There were two writing tables, just as you had instructed me to specify on the application form: one for prose (against the wall where the computer stood) and one for poetry (by the window). There were two bedrooms also: a small cabin on the ground floor, with a view upon the rear end of the Sint Nicolaas Church, and a larger one on the upper floor. But I could not write a single word.*

I impaled the letter on the pegs in the file and clicked the clamp into place. After all the ruffling of drums in the opening lines, nothing unusual here in this description of a space. And 'astonishment'? By what could he possibly have been astonished if not by the enormous, undeserved privilege of landing, gratis, for three months in such quarters. And he ends up in intensive care, certainly not as a result of *tremendum et fascinans*, but out of utter laziness. I was livid when I thought of all the forms and testimonials and special words whispered to my colleagues in Amsterdam asking to give this student a chance. I ripped Kasper Olwagen's letter from my file and thrust it into a drawer full of speeding tickets and bills.

Eight months later, as I was reviewing the translation of my novel, I received notice of a package from the post office. Kasper, I knew, had returned in the meantime; the university administration had informed me that he had personally de-registered. But he had not had the decency to come and see me or explain himself. I fetched the package at the post office in Die Boord only a week after the third and final notice was delivered. It was wrapped in brown paper, laced up in four strings of white cotton line, with a knob of red wax on the knot at the back. When I opened it in the kitchen, audio cassettes clattered down on my feet, sixteen TDK cassettes of sixty minutes each. With them, the dummy of my novel, already published by that time – I had given it to Kasper for good luck on the day of his departure for Amsterdam, a white model book, firmly bound, two hundred and fifty unprinted blank

Riporto

29 Radonich
    S. Ulrich
    Primavera
    Morgenstern
    Panaticke p. Cassa
31 R. G. franca

Cap. di Po...

...

Sala Cassa S.T.
Panaticke per Cass...

Piazza d'Armi — Piazza Giuseppe Verdi — Via del Prato — Via Ugo Foscolo — Via XX Settembre

Giorio

Comunali Gao

n 8 wilson

Hoenig E Nanari
G. Pilotti
Martini
G. Stokel E Febarla
Villa G. Cadorni
Gallis
G. Campari
G. Caux
bradvella
G. Pansini

G. Angei S.A.
G. Guadagni
Papo Co.
Given
E. Brunol

pages. At the front I had written: 'To Kasper, for your ideas, for the letters dropped upon the streets by the gods.' He had looked at me with trepidation after reading the inscription, his hand on his heart, nostrils twitching, as if I had handed him something malodorous.

In the package was a note:

Dear Professor Van Niekerk: The heart guards its sorrow, here as in Amsterdam. Included please find what has become of your phantom book, now called The Logbook of a Swan Whisperer. *The tapes should amuse you even more. All details therein have been deleted, all ideas removed. Farewell to the worlds of will and representation! Kind regards, Kasper.*

I kicked at the cassettes on the kitchen floor. Swan whisperer? I had heard of a horse whisperer, but what in God's name was a swan whisperer?

I opened my dummy book, at least one half of which was covered with writing in tiny fountain-pen script, showing columns with headings giving location, time, and action, a firm chronology of dates in the rows: 11 December 2001 up to 15 January 2002. 'Location' yielded mostly references to some bridge or other along the canal belt, while under 'action' were a few cryptic notes, descriptions of some occultist events. Let me read you a few typical inscriptions: 11 December 'Bridge Prinsegracht, Utrecht Street. Swan whisperer: posture especially stiff today, supplication with murmuring, hands lifted, rope-ladder down to the water, three swans from under the bridge.' Or 'Bridge Lauriergracht. Swan whisperer looks up to the firmament, shakes coat out over the water, murmurs constantly, one swan from under the bridge.' Repeatedly: bridge, gestures, swans; gestures, murmurings, swans, bridge; the same phrases over and over.

The cassettes were from a more recent period, labelled 1 to 16 with dates going from 5 March to 17 May 2002. My cassette player was broken, but I could imagine what they would contain: names of grasses, rocks, insects, alphabetically entered. The sorts of lists you would expect of Mr Stranger.

The Olwagen mock-up of my book prompted me to open that drawer into which I had shoved his letter. 'Drawer whisperer,' I grumbled, because it was so full of rubbish that it would not open. I had to flatten out the letter page by page before I could read it.

Esteemed listeners, imagine, if you will, a young man from the swanless south, an alien in a world city, a struggling writer, alone, anguished, neurotic. He breaks down, as is to be expected. There he lies, in a foreign hospital, his tongue feeling thick, his hands shaking from the medication administered, and he writes his teacher a letter about what has allegedly happened to him. Pure fantasy? A cover-up of the true situation? A hidden confession? A concealment of failure? Or a disguising of fears and hankerings? Whichever it may have been, he hands in a logbook, evidence in support of the validity of his story. Let us give him the chance to set his stage:

It was, Professor, as they say here in Dutch, the donkere dagen voor de Kerst (the dark days before Christmas). *For weeks I had been eating nothing but baked beans from tins. At night I did not go to bed, but fell asleep on the red sofa in front of the television. I had ceased to go out, spent entire mornings at the window-pane, rocking my head to and fro so that the quay, the docks, the traffic in the street all appeared to me in turn, in different distortions. I would blow on the glass to write words on it.* BLAME, PENANCE, LOSS, SHAME. *These great black bells in my tower, the reason why I could never write anything. Just once I wrote:* BEAUTY, BREATH, SONG *– and started crying.*

Then I awoke one morning, like a prince in the mist – a great mist of the night, frozen to the elms as in a fairytale, pure lacework in the trees alongside the quay. I blew upon the window-pane and on it I wrote a line of verse that I recollected from somewhere: 'Perhaps my whisper was born before my lips.'

You always said, Professor, that we are here to be called to, to be called upon, to be summoned into existence. Why, once the lesson is fulfilled, is the master ever absent from the pupil?

When I erased the line of poetry with the tip of my finger, there he stood, framed in the mist of my breath, across the canal under a portico, with snow-white hair and a bag in his hand, and then he walked forward and leaned over the side of the bridge. He was in his late forties, maybe fifty, scruffy, homeless. Fluff protruded from his coat. His lips were moving. I followed his gaze, to the unruffled water beneath the bridge. What did he see there?

He straightened up, still murmuring, hands in the air like a conductor before the orchestra strikes up. Then he gave the first beat. And there, from under the bridge, swam two swans towards him, majestically, parading their necks, as if they belonged to him.

It was as if I saw for the very first time what a swan was: feathery raiment of milk-white glass, a neck blown in a dream of fire, a vase under sail, bound to its reflection; masked twins, breast to breast in a dance, dark music in the webs of their feet.

The swan caller untied his bundle, and removed a rope ladder with which he let himself down to the deck of a small sailboat docked there against the quay.

A god in the crib of the rime-white dawn.

On his stomach, with his hands stretched out over the water, he called to the birds, their tails wagging, their heads close to his. Orpheus on the bank. That I could, with my finger, write a line by a forgotten poet, and have it leap from window-pane to canal embankment and change into a swan whisperer...? The heart delights in such fortuitousness.

I didn't buy it. Do you? I could guess what was going to happen next. And I was right.

Kasper falls under the spell of the so-called 'swan whisperer' – which translates as: he falls for his own fantasy about the swan whisperer – and unto us a story is born. Daily he follows him through the city and at every bridge bears witness to this homeless man's swan ritual. Priest-like, the man lifts his hands, murmurs some magic word or formula; the swans appear as though summoned, from under the bridge, whereupon the swan master descends his rope ladder to bewhisper them.

There follows a passage I cannot resist reading to you:

I hear you at this point, Professor. You're thinking: This is not about to become interesting, Kasper. Your story contains: 1. A writer with writer's block. 2. A pair of binoculars. 3. A maladjusted vagrant with a swan fixation. This is insufficient material, it smells of parable, you'll have to enjoin your characters to become involved with one another, as nothing can convince an author to jettison symbols as effectively as the establishing of relations between characters. I know, dear prof, that, given your limitations, you will be unable to read this cry for help, that you will appraise it simply as a piece of writing, nothing more. Yet writing

and living coincide completely in this letter, and involvement ensued the
very next day, when I spotted the man across the quay. I followed him
down his rope ladder onto the boat. What did he smell of? Of compost?
Ever the eager pupil, I lay down beside him on my stomach on the deck.
Would you not have done the same? Would you not have endeavoured to
determine what he was whispering to the swans? Could it be scripture,
from the water-line of their flanks? Or runes from the swan-depths?

With or without scripture, dear listeners, Kasper takes the
vagrant home, feeds him. A young, unsociable South African man,
an overbred neurotic afraid of germs, offers accommodation to a
grimy maladjusted stranger. And as Kasper the philosopher takes
pains to impress upon his reader, this patient of his was a blank
page, a tight-lipped stray. (What hero would want to take care of
an eloquent invalid? No, the man could not, or would not, speak.)
His gaze was dull and vacant. He was torpid and lethargic. He
didn't even know how to use the bathroom.

I removed his soiled coat and worn-out trousers and shirt. He had on no
underwear, and no socks inside his boots. He was very thin. There was
a brown layer around his ankles and wrists and neck. His frayed clothes
stuck as a crust over his entire body, forming a kind of flaky silver fleece
with his body hair. In his crotch the hair formed a thick, caked mat. His
sex was shrunken away. The hair under his arms was long and white.
His toenails and fingernails were long and badly torn.

I put on the dishwashing gloves from the kitchen drawer and had him
sit on a stool in the shower. I sponged his body down, then soaped him
with disinfectant, washing him carefully with a soft cloth.

Why did cleaning him feel like trespassing? Can you explain that
to me, professor? You, who understand these things so well? Why such
sorrow as I washed this damaged individual? I was grateful for the steam
through which my tears could run without being noticed. I helped him
stand up, pressing my forehead against his chest to keep him upright,
using my body as a prop to turn him round in the cubicle.

I was scared to strip him of his shell. But would it not be more
deadly to fail to try: deadlier for him, and even deadlier for me. Do you
understand? I caught a glimpse of our ghostly figures in the mirror, he
with his hand on my shoulder, and was startled by the effect of my
ablutions. Where the crust came off, his skin was tender, with inflamed

萬像渾入鴻濛界　中夜拜受命

推移大曆天開子　歲□□先天斗柄指

垂衣至化像乾坤　龍宮□元消息與歲運

開物元年視萬理　鳳□□珠旒溯天軌

庖犧甲曆不盡妙　三□□暦數推來癸亥禩

玉杓前霄乾象視　□□□□終始

周天星運六十度　星培□侯命甘欽

莩一干支閏逢是　六衢明廷臣有□□曆數推來癸亥禩

陰陽四時互消長　回環歲序太初天

星宿千年迭遷徙　敬受人時常在此

道神大化六氣調　玄功不獨肄作算

天地人文心暗揣　妙理寧同沮誦史

○見日月星辰之像命大撓作甲子　二所杜全漢老

讀魯仲連蹈海書疑古所謂仙不死二中壯元鄭可
會試

海上孤鳥蒼〻畫三洲虛月影子隱　瑤宮司命𠀤
篁林曉跡齊諧書六國先天蹤跡餘　仲連清篇徵

滄園讀燈照舂漢清都白雲誰家奐　仙初不死當
仙海千古無疑余茂陵秋風驪峀如山亦巻

甲橫烈士一島是
罤連此任江處茶

red patches on the flanks and round his waist – something that looked like scabies. Or shingles? Psoriasis?

'Het ziet er niet so best uit,' I said, 'maar maakt u zich geen zorgen, wij komen er wel uit.' ('It doesn't look so good, but don't worry, we'll figure it out.')

What next for Kasper in this fairytale, learned colleagues? He purchases salves and oils and balms at the apothecary. He buys new white clothes at Hema, a coat and shoes, and the most nutritious ingredients for the invalid's meals. He pushes his two tables together, the poetry and the prose, covering them in white towels, raising his reading lamp like in an operating theatre, then laying on it the naked swan whisperer in order to nurse him from head to toe, three times a day for a fortnight.

I could read no further.

This was to be the third time I interrupted my reading of his letter. I stashed it with my teaching materials, along with the white dummy; it had occurred to me that I could use it to explain to my students the problems with magical realism. Not that I ever did this, choosing rather to give my house a thorough going-over, have the painting and pruning done and the squirrels removed from inside the roof, set a trap for the mouse, let my wrist heal.

But then, about one month later, restoration in full swing, the letter all but forgotten (his book unread, his cassettes unplayed), I received a third shipment of an oddly bulky envelope in my letter-box. I stood surrounded by painters from Wonder Wall in their white overalls as I tore open the envelope. It was filled with sand: a handful of pure white sand falling to my feet. I stepped back to reveal my two dark footprints on the paving. I sent the workmen home for the day, then checked the back of the envelope: no sender, just a scribble, made with something like a stick of charcoal: the name *Dwarsrivier*.

Why *Dwarsrivier* – *Diagonal River*? Some allegorical joke? Perhaps Kasper's letter held a clue? Should I take a closer look at his logbook, listen to his cassettes? I gathered all his consignments onto the kitchen table. First, I picked up his letter and read on from page twenty, where I had stopped the last time. Let me summarise for you.

After a month of skin treatments, the drifter's hide was healed, his hair was cut, his scent was pleasantly human. But this was not enough. Kasper was determined the swan whisperer would speak. He was jealous of him, of his art of communicating with the 'birds of the underworld' (as he called them). At night, he watched over the dozing vagabond with his logbook in hand, in case the man might talk in his sleep; but all he heard was the ticking of the radiator, the rain pattering against the windows, the bell of Sint Nicolaas. If he could just get him to open his mouth, if only to say at dinner 'Please pass the salt,' then he could question him about swan charming.

Asking for salt, ladies and gentlemen? I had to smile, for such verisimilitude was incompatible with Kasper's story. As this letter was addressed to me, the student whisperer (if you will), it made me increasingly feel as if Kasper were constructing an argument, leading the man towards utterance along a *via dolorosa* with a fixed itinerary.

I never replied. This is the first time I have ever spoken of my neglect.

Let me return to the story. How did Mister Philanthropist attempt to goad his wayward guest into speech? First, he sat him down in front of the television for hours on end, trying to incite him with images of broken knees in Kenya, with the terror of the long knives in Zimbabwe, with the mourning polar bears of the North Pole, with the smouldering trees of the Amazon; when this didn't work, he had him climb through the roof hatch to view the swan and the harp in the constellations, the tears of Orpheus in the West; and when this too failed to work, he had him listen to every romantic swansong he could lay his hands on in the library – Grieg, Sibelius, Tchaikovsky. All for nought. Neither the terrors of our own time nor the eternal signature of the firmament, neither the dated melodies of the Romantic era nor a glass of Burgundy – nothing could untie this tramp's tongue. Kasper considered taking him to a psychiatrist, or to an ear, nose and throat specialist. One morning he examined the swan whisperer's mouth himself, only to find there a healthy light-red tongue, the clapper firmly strapped to the root. He continues:

I shone light into the back of his throat. The tonsils hung in the uvula like two small bells. I ran my index finger along the roof of his mouth whose ridges reminded me of a harp.

Yet harps would not resound, at least not in Kasper's writing. What he noted down were rows and columns, records and registrations, in shorthand throughout. At the entry for 5 January 2003, I found the following written out in full sentences, the sole semblance of self-reflection.

Swannyboy's standing like a statue behind my chair where I'm trying to write, been like that for hours, as if he's supervising me. I pretend not to know he's there, but I'm listening. What is it I'm hearing? Just the sounds of the city? The sibilance of his blood? Or my own? He doesn't know that I can see his reflection in the glass of the picture on the wall, I can see his lips moving, and I move my pen over the page as well as I can, in time with what I imagine him to be saying. Of what does my pen remind me? Of the graphite bar in a weather station, registering all moisture and wind and cloud movements and recording them on a roll of graph paper.

And this is followed by rows and rows of sounds, the phonological patterns of Afrikaans. Certain examples show the influence of the Khoi languages. *Spak, grak, spal, malk, olk, skolk* and then *mrie !krie krakadouw*. Some of them were put together at random and arranged into what I can only call *sound limericks*. Transcriptions of what Kasper thought the swan whisperer was saying: swan whisperings. And the sound of the language of swans?

> *Rie mrie, rapuu,*
> *kriep, !tewiek, miruu,*
> *tohoe wa bohoe*
> *askla mor usa,*
> *pierok griemok sklahoe.*

Although I do enjoy nonsense verse, I really did not feel like being taken for a fool by a psychotic student in search of a mother. I smacked the book shut. Look, professor, he seemed to be telling me: a deaf and dumb schizophrenic can teach me more about the art of writing than you ever could!

I should probably have known it was not innocent. One year later I happened upon the phrase "tohoe wa bohoe" in a book about the Pentateuch, Hebrew for the formless void, from Genesis. I still do not know what to make of this.

Now I must relate something that one in my line of work would rather forget, as it may serve as clarification. It concerns an incident from the time when Kasper was still registered as a student, the only time he dared contradict me. I had summoned him for feedback on his latest piece of writing. I wished to conclude briskly. Barely had he taken his seat when I fired away. 'Drop the metaphysics, Kasper,' I said, 'drop the ideas, write what readers want, a juicy story about your hometown, a tale of unwanted newcomers, gang violence, dogfights, highway robbery, shebeens, self-importance, adultery, braaivleis, family feuds, Maggie Laubser, and piety. Call it *The Sorrows of Rustling Rivers.*'

Kasper's eyes glazed over, his voice was thin when he replied. 'And with a self-important local author as narrator?' he said. 'The days of good-natured local realism are over, in case you hadn't noticed, even when it's dressed up in metafictional drag. If I were to write prose one day, it would consist of street reports, sidewalk anthropology, recorded from a perspective of distant sympathy. Cut and dried.'

Small bubbles of spittle were visible at the corners of his mouth. His hand was inside his blazer, but he did not remove his pen.

'Fiction,' he continued, with his tongue dragging more than usual, 'fiction can no longer console us. The terrors of our fatherland rob the narrative imagination of desire and determination. Imagining is no longer possible. We have to become brutal collectors of facts, no longer storytellers, we have to become archivists of the unimaginable brutalities of our country. From what we write our readers will gather fear and empathy, perhaps even entertainment and knowledge.'

I was finally learning something from a student, though I was not about to admit that I was impressed. To be honest, I was jealous of what I recognised as an angle for a new literary movement in Afrikaans literature, which had become so woefully stuck in adventure and self-portrayal.

'Mr Olwagen,' I said, 'I fear you feign bravery. When I look at you, I see no brutalist, I see an aesthete. I do not see lists of necklace murders, raped children, murdered geriatrics, armed robberies. What I do see, rather, are lists of fauna and flora,

Lehman's love grass, heart-seed love grass, stagger grass, fountain grass, quaking grass . . . Shouldn't you rather stay true to your own nature? You read Adorno's aesthetic theories, yet I fail to detect in you a critical analyst or a taste for satirical commentary on your fatherland. I look at your twitching nostrils and your hand on your heart and I see someone who feels overwhelmed, weak, scared, alone, unwilling to give himself a death sentence in sixteen lines, unlike the Osip Mandelstam you so admire, who did it with his poem about everybody's beloved Onkel Stalin. Or like Breytenbach in his poem about the butcher. Like no poet today would dare to write about Robert Mugabe. You have a lazy tongue, Olwagen. You are a symptom of the problem besetting progressive intellectuals in this country: politically correct pose on the one hand and escapist actions on the other. Get a life – that's my suggestion.'

He was staring at me with that smouldering gaze of his, but I did not return the look.

'Be honest,' I said, 'how do you want to be a sidewalk anthropologist on any interesting pavement in this country today without an armed bodyguard by your side?' And when I got no reaction: 'Your kind has been outlawed in this country,' I went on, 'there's always someone who needs a bowtie when a pig is being butchered.' I stood up behind my desk. He had to grasp this clearly, I would leave no room for misunderstanding. 'Mr Olwagen,' I said, 'do you want to know what I see when I look at you? I see someone who wants to banish himself to the sticks, yes, way beyond the backveld, who in unblemished nature would become an architect of the exalted moment, a sculptor in the amber of words. You wish to become a human animal in your language, the way a genet is himself only in the undergrowth. I see your dictum written all over your imposing forehead: *The only subversive deed remaining in a superficial, brutalised society is the cultivation of the intimate discomfort of the lyric.* True or false? Or would you formulate your escapist desires differently?'

I could see that he was in difficulty. But what teacher has never upset a student? Not that one intends to, but there's little remedy if a student feels crushed.

This is not how an educator should act.

10

Let me return to the present. I took out my atlas and, lo and behold, there it was, no allegories here, a real Dwarsrivier did exist, in the Cederberg Mountains, a farm belonging to the Nieuwoudt clan, closest post-office: Clanwilliam. I took dustpan and brush, swept up the sand, poured it back into the envelope. For the purposes of the present lecture I have transferred it into this hourglass.

You have to understand the situation: Kasper's letter from hospital was nothing less than a user's manual. I was obliged to return to this letter repeatedly in order to make sense of the ensuing packages. Was this his plan for vengeance? Or had I been snared by an implausibly captivating story? You see, I still didn't believe in the swan whisperer. I sat at my kitchen table, downing cup after cup of coffee, leafing through Kasper's densely written pages. There was a teeth-pulling scene on page fifty. *'Perhaps the man has dental difficulties,'* Kasper writes, *'and that explains why he won't talk.'* He took his lodger to the dentist, where three teeth were pulled, and numerous fillings administered. Then follows the part of his letter that got me thinking that perhaps my former student really had experienced something preposterous.

On the night of 20 January, after the teeth were pulled, I was woken by a draught against my neck. The swan whisperer was out of bed, in front of the open window in his nightclothes, his arms raised. I slipped down the stairs behind him. On the canal in front of my apartment there were not one or two, but thousands of swans, covering the length of the Geldersekade, nodding and swishing – necks bowing, stretching, curving, a script in motion – a white cursive dance of swans over the black ink of the canal. They came swimming from beneath the bridge, from the Oosterdok they swarmed, the air alive with the whirring of their wings. With their long necks set back, they landed in the mass of white, flapping and splashing. I was astonished at the steadily growing congregation of pedunculate necks, the feathers royally displayed in a massive nocturnal plume, the surface of the water astir under the blue light emanating from the Liebherr cranes. This is how it must have looked when the gods herded the swans together to pull the sled of Orpheus.

Professor, what does one call a drift of swans in Afrikaans? A drifsel? Could one call them a swath? Or a drum? A longing, a sin, or a shame of swans?

I didn't return to the flat that evening, I wandered round the city, too astounded at the spectacle of swans, all my doubts, any residual reservations about this drifter summarily eliminated. He was a genius. Autistic, perhaps, but a genius. Would he take me as his apprentice? Or as the scribe of his whisperings? No, and I understood that I was to be neither his saviour nor his translator. Nor his lover, however sweet that might have been as an ending.

By six in the morning, tired and cold and hungry, I finally knew what to do. I had to return to the flat and switch on the kettle. At a quarter to seven I had to knock on his door, open the curtains, and touch his shoulder to wake him, just as I had done every morning for the past ten weeks. I had to sit on the chair beside his bed and drink coffee with him in the sleepy silence, while we listened to the city slowly awakening, the train wheels scouring the tracks, the siren in the Oosterdok announcing another workday. Together we had to sit there, while the morning glow filled the room and a lone sparrow chirped in the gutter on the roof, waiting for the bells to strike seven – the Oude Kerk on De Wallen always first, then, after two strokes, the Zuiderkerk, and then promptly the closer clangour of Sint Nicolaas, as its dorsal fins were being sketched by the morning light. And all of this I would be able to do without any worry for the first time that morning, because I had understood that, after everything, and despite his unusual abilities, I had simply become his friend, the friend of this singular man.

Seated there at my kitchen table I now knew, without a doubt, that all of this was true. Poignant and true. Because when Kasper returned to the flat that morning with his newfound insight, it was too late: his friend was gone, missing, rope-ladder and all.

And there's more. Page sixty-three.

He was disconsolate, Kasper explains, utterly inconsolable. Just when he finally realised what was important about the swan whisperer – not his Orphic arts, but his simple bodily presence as a housemate – his friend disappeared. Days on end Kasper looked for him, up and down the swan route. He searched every night shelter, enquired at every welfare society, asked every vendor of a *Daklozenkrant* – the homeless person's newspaper: 'Heeft u een man gezien met wit haar en een touwladder?' ('Have you seen a man with white hair and a rope ladder?'). He distributed flyers throughout the city: 'VRIEND VERMIST' ('FRIEND MISSING').

塵同　　　　　　　　　唐。

非非來　　　　非其　　　雨

皐罪。虎

未作戀娘。　　　　良人

然殊甲冑　　　胃既

賣商

口是為　刅創同

來依井井方　創

乔刅畔無　又是

乔瘡　登倉　有頭

殊　祭　廣慶

In the course of his search, Kasper himself becomes a drifter. Day and night, in wind and rain, he walks in the threadbare coat, wearing the boots of the swan whisperer. And here we find splendid descriptions of Amsterdam, the reflections, the gables, the elms, the trams, always with the notion: I'm no longer seeking inspiration or authorial fulfilment, I'm looking for my friend, and every street corner and every reflection and every bridge speaks of my longing. Kasper tells – and here the angels begin to dance as Kasper becomes a writer – of how he lingered at every bridge where he used to find the swan whisperer, raising his hands in the air and murmuring: 'What did I do wrong to lose my mate?'

Let me read you his final page.

I believed I'd spotted him once – white hair in front of me on the bustling sidewalk – and I was gripped by the conviction that I should not cry out or run up to him, that if he were to turn round and see me, I would be lost. I sensed that I myself had been followed for some time, and by someone who seemed to recognise me. I was part of a procession, a silent convoy of the urban lost and looking, all of us connected at the wrist by an endless black ribbon, all of us thinking that perhaps we have found a missing person, but afraid to make this hope known, afraid of disappointment, choosing rather the solace of a community of like-minded individuals, the consolation of not being alone, of belonging to the least breakable brotherhood on earth: of those who have stayed on, who have survived, who have been left behind.

And so, dear listeners, Kasper ends where he began, in the portico across from his own home where first he saw the whisperer. He falls asleep there, hungry and exhausted, at a degree or two below freezing. He slips into a coma. The city police pick him up and deliver him to hospital, as he puts it: *Without name, without papers, with only my story and the need to tell it to the one person on earth who might understand.*

After two months and no further unusual packages, I bought a new cassette player, and travelled to the Cederberg Mountains. The deeper I went into the Gydo pass, straight through towards Clanwilliam, the more I knew I was on track. I found the Dwarsrivier farm easily enough and unpacked at a campground called Sanddrif. The sand in Kasper's envelope matched exactly what I found by the river there.

That night in my tent I listened to his tapes, fifty-three recitations. I concluded that they were poems, recorded near to running water or waving grass, as though Kasper had wished to provide his voice with a kind of pedal point: not a bold bass pedal as in Bach, but rustling, murmuring, as though time were an instrument played by the transparent fingers of grass and water. I walked up and down the river for days, my cassette player in hand, until I found what I was seeking: that specific minor murmuring of water over flat rock provided by a small whirlpool, and a patch of reeds with white plumes that rustled like Chinese cymbals. To the background of these sounds Kasper had chosen to record his voice.

Pale, oversensitive Kasper, how cold he must have been in those bare gorges in winter, beside that dark stream. Did he hang his bowtie on a reed? His waistcoat on an aloe? Did he empty his fountain pen on the sand?

However closely I listened – and, ladies and gentlemen, I am still listening, shall never stop listening – I could not discern the words of his poems, if that's even what they were. I could make out the firm commencement of the theme, and then the countermovement, varied somewhat in vowels and consonants, propped and built up by repetition and refrains, magnificent edifices of sound. I could catch rhythms, variations, the length and cadence of the lines, their inversions and elongations and enrichments; climaxes, accelerations, decelerations. I could catch the tone and feel of each recitation, sometimes elegiac and legato, sometimes exuberant, often painfully ecstatic, always songlike. I could grasp the argument of the sounds, or rather the research through sound for possibilities of development or variation of the central theme. But never the meaning.

My work, I know, is measured out for the remainder of my life. I am the real dummy, you see, the mock-up professor, and god only knows who is writing in me. Someone pinned a tongue on me. My just deserts, I would say, if it is my missing student or his missing friend who has done it. But I won't give up, it's bad enough that two people have vanished without a trace. I sit in my yard and the seasons pass over me. I no longer write novels: I have come to see myself as a *translator*.

I study the lists of compound sounds that Kasper entered in my book – that empty parting gift to him. Using these, I make one translation after another of his sound poems. As soon as I finish one, I read it in unison with the sound patterns in the corresponding recording, and I keep working on it until it matches his voice as closely as possible. Much is lost in this process; perhaps something is gained. I drop the adjectives, I delete the ideas, I barely attach the sounds to meaning, because meaning is incidental. What matters are the material words. They must become like grains of sand, inconsequential in weight, sweet, white, dry: sand that does not care if it slips through the fingers. Twice a year, I go to the Cederberg Mountains, to that whirlpool, to that patch of marsh reeds, and there I read my latest translations out loud, in the hope that the water and the plumes will keep whispering them, perhaps whisper them through to him, if he is still somewhere out there.

Shall I share my latest attempt with you? I dedicate it to my lost student, the one who taught me everything a writer should be – which is, of course, quite distinct from what a writer should write.

Oggend van 'n Waterfiskaal
Allagot! geglip uit die knukkels
van hierdie kant se koskans- en hansmaker,
wip die waterfiskaal die oggendkier in
kaneeeeeel van verbasing op sy bors,
onder die kruidnagelkloudjies die rinkink-rulle
spiksplinterspuwende Dwarsriviersand,
tinktuuuuuur van manelkwik geveer op sy flanke,
strak in die frak die keil platgekam
akkelief hy oor die akkers tot die waterkant, kyk!
triljarrrrrrrrde klein en groot fiskale innie spiekspieghel –
hokaai kohorte kansvatters –
wat hy konter met pronkstad akimbo,
knipstert na die kindlig in die oewerkrui,
en wegstaan, kykso, eeeeene ollewagen onderbaadjie,
hy is die slim en innigste godontglipper
hier in die prilwilde hoogmakerson
!tewiek in sy keel sit sy roepnaam !tewiek
soos 'n klok in die bergkut ketoooools
van die mondsagte môre.

Morning of the Southern Boubou
Holy crack! slipped from the knuckles
of this side's foodfiddler and domesticator,
the shrike flits through the daybreak's crevice,
amaaaazed at the spice of his cinnamon chest,
under his clove-claws crumbles the rock 'n' roll rippin'
spick 'n' span spewing crossriversands,
tincture of peck flecked on his coattails and flanks,
fixed in his frock, the tophat caruncled
he frolicks over acres to the edge, now look!
triiiiiiillions of big and small shrikes in the looking glass –
ho now, you cohorts of chancers in the ripples –
that he counters, coxcombry akimbo,
flicktailing the kidlight in the riverine herb,
and sidesteps, looknow, weeeeeaving the olwagen waistcoat,
he is the one and only goddodger
here in the tendertipped sacredmakersun,
!tooweak in his throttle sits his petname !tooweak
like a bell in the mountcunt aroooooooused
by the mouthsoft morn.

COLOPHON

THE CAHIERS SERIES   ·   NUMBER 25
ISBN: 978-1-90963110-6

Printed by Principal Colour, Paddock Wood, on
Neptune Unique (text) and Chagall (dust jacket).
Set in Giovanni Mardersteig's Monotype Dante.

Series Editor: Dan Gunn
Associate Series Editor: Daniel Medin
Design: Sylph Editions Design

Text: ©Marlene van Niekerk, 2015
Images: © William Kentridge, 2015

With thanks to Jan Steyn. And with special thanks
to Marie Donnelly, as well as the Tides Foundation,
for their generous support.

CENTER FOR WRITERS & TRANSLATORS
THE AMERICAN UNIVERSITY OF PARIS

SYLPH EDITIONS, LONDON | 2015

THE AMERICAN
UNIVERSITY 50
of PARIS YEARS

center for writers and translators

SYLPH
EDITIONS

www.aup.edu   ·   www.sylpheditions.com

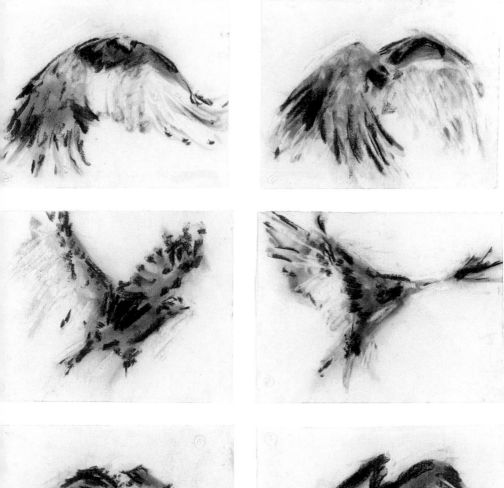

KENTRIDGE
2007